RICHARD SCARRY

Great Big Schoolhouse

First published in Great Britain in 1977 by HarperCollins Children's Books.
This edition published in Great Britain in 2007 by HarperCollins Children's Books.
HarperCollins Children's Books is a division of HarperCollins Publishers Ltd.

1 3 5 7 9 10 8 6 4 2
ISBN-13: 978-0-00-718946-5
ISBN-10: 0-00-718946-X

RICHARD SCARRY

Great Big Schoolhouse

HarperCollins *Children's Books*

Getting Ready For School

Huckle's mother woke him up.
"It's time to get up for school," she said.
"Why do I have to go to school?" asked Huckle.
"All children go to school to learn how to read
and write," said his mother. "You want to be able
to read and write don't you? Now please get up."

blanket

Huckle got up. He yawned and rubbed the sleep
out of his eyes. He walked to the bathroom.

mirror

sink

towel   soap

He washed his face
with soap and warm water.

pyjamas

toothpaste

He brushed his teeth.

comb

He combed his hair
with cold water.

braces

underpants

shirt   suit jacket   overcoat   play jacket   overalls   raincoat   rain hat

shoes   gloves   mittens   rubber hat

socks

Then Huckle got dressed. This is NOT the way to put on your trousers, Huckle!

bacon
eggs
cup
teapot
saucer
spoon
glass
brief case
tablecloth
fork
knife

Mother Cat served hot cereal to Huckle for his breakfast.
Lowly Worm called on his way to school.
"Hurry up or you will be late for school," he said.

"LATE! My goodness! I am late for work," said Father Cat. He picked
up his briefcase and ran. Oh dear! He picked up the tablecloth, too!

Mother Cat walked with Huckle to the school bus stop.
Honk! Honk! The school bus came
to take the children to school.

SCHOOL

SCHOOL
BUS
STOP

SCHOOL BUS

Riding on the School Bus

black engine

red and green coach

Every day Huckle rides to school in his orange school bus.
He sees many colourful things. Everything has a colour.
What colour is the fisherman's suit?

purple jeep

manhole

SCHOOL BUS

street

red motorcycle

Gorilla Bananas and his yellow Bananamobile

orange aeroplane

white ambulance with red crosses

railway crossing gate

crossing guard

traffic light

blue sign

red fire engine

yellow crossing

green taxi

fisherman

tugboat

TAXI

brown delivery van

bridge

river

GO RIGHT

The School

This is Huckle's school. The school bus stopped at the
school. The school bell rang. It was time for school
to begin. But what was all that
noise outside?

postman

weather vane

bell

clock
tower

CENTRAL
SCHOOL

office

playground

policeman

school crossing guard

chimney sweep

school library

classroom

classroom

classroom

classroom

classroom

classroom

doctor's office

HATS

SCHOOL BUS

SCHOOL

Why, it was Joe, the caretaker!
As usual, he was late for school.

balloon

alphabet

string

Aa Aa | Bb Bb | Cc Cc | Dd Da

clock

bell

wall

notice board

calendar

teacher

SEPTEMBER
SUN MON TUES WED THU FRI SAT
1 2 3 4 5
6 7 8 9 10 11 12
13 14 15 16 17 18 19
20 21 22 23 24 25 26
27 28 29 30

umbrella

overshoes

pupils

desk

The Classroom

This is Huckle's classroom. And behind the desk sits
Miss Honey, his teacher. Every morning the pupils say,
"Good morning, Miss Honey." And every morning, she says,
"Good morning, children. My, don't you look bright
and fresh this morning!" She always says that.

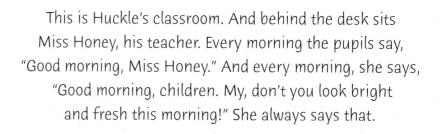

Ee *Ee*   Ff *Ff*   Gg *Gg*   Hh *Hh*   Ii *Ii*

paper aeroplane

spider pupil

blind

blackboard

window pane

spelling lesson

cat
dog
worm

arithmetic lesson

$$\begin{array}{r} 2 \\ +\ 2 \\ \hline 4 \end{array}$$

a pupil who is
late for school

wastepaper basket

stool

window sill

table

Huckle's chair

Lowly Worm's chair

pencil sharpener

paste pot

ruler

paper clips

blackboard duster

rubber

pencil box

workbook

chalk

storybook

pencil

marker pen

drawing pins

Richard Scarry's
What Do
People Do,
All Day?

ball-point pen

push pins

LEARNING THE ALPHABET

Aa Bb Cc Dd Ee Ff Gg Hh Ii Jj Kk Ll
Mm Nn Oo Pp Qq Rr Ss Tt Uu Vv Ww Xx Yy Zz

Each day Miss Honey teaches her class something new.
Today she was going to teach them the alphabet. She gave each child
a card with one of the letters of the alphabet on it. Everyone tried
to think of words that began with the letters on their cards.

yum yum!

A is the first letter of the **a**lphabet.
Arthur Pig brought **an a**pple for the teacher.
He **a**lso brought one for his friend, Lowly Worm.

apple

broom

bowl

book

bench

"**B**ananas Gorilla! Take that **B**ananamobile **b**ack
outside where it **b**elongs!" said Miss Honey.
"And please eat your **b**reakfast at home!"

boot

banana

crayon

car

card

Cc

Charles Anteater drew a **c**ar with his **c**rayon.
He showed it to the **c**lass.

Dd

drawer

dirt

desk

Donald Walrus **d**anced up and **d**own on his **d**esk.
Did you see his **d**rawer pop out?

eyeglasses

ear-rings

electric bulb

egg cup

empty purse

envelope

egg

broken egg

Ee

Elizabeth **e**mptied her purse
and found some **e**ar-rings.
She put them on. They
were **e**xtra-heavy.

furniture

fountain

Frances Raccoon showed the children her doll's
furniture. Lowly Worm turned on the bath tap
and pretended to be a fountain.

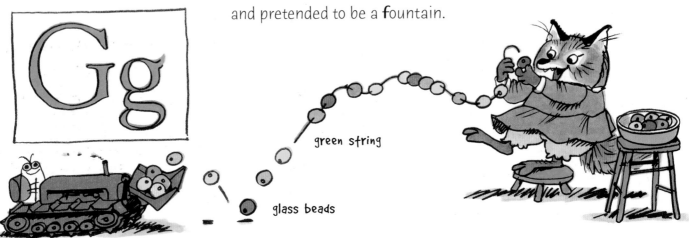

Gg

green string

glass beads

Gloria Fox strung glass beads on a green string.
She forgot that there are two ends to a piece
of string. Bugdozer gathered up the runaway beads.

HONK!

hat   head

Hh

keep your nose up!

Huckle blew hard on his horn. Lowly was
hiding in it. Now Lowly knows how to fly!

Ii

I can fly as straight
as an arrow!

Indian

Irving Goat is pretending
he is an Indian.

orange juice

Jj

jam

Jimmy Crocodile spread orange juice
on his bread and poured jam in his glass.
Now just a minute! Isn't that wrong?

Kk

kerchief

how do you get it to come out?

ketchup

sharp
kitchen
knives

bread knife

kettle

Kathy is wearing a scarf. Lowly is shaking up the
ketchup. Kathy is showing us things that are used
in the kitchen. Never touch sharp kitchen knives.

Ll

laundry

All right, Lowly! How many things can
you name that begin with the letter 'L'?

ladder

lemon

log

loaf of
bread

lantern

leaf

lunch box

lamp

letter
to post

lettuce

Very good, Lowly! Now, please take your seat.

Mm

melon

Mildred Hippo is a **m**agician.
She can **m**ake things disappear.
She put a **m**elon in her **m**outh.
She **m**unched on it.
It disappeared! **M**mmm ! Good !
My ! What a **m**arvellous trick !

nut

nose (or trunk)

Nn

napkin

new suit

Ned's turn was **n**ext. He balanced
a **n**ut on his **n**ose. He wore
a **n**apkin because he did
not want to get any crumbs
on his **n**ew suit.

Oo

orange

oil

onion

oboe

oak
leaf

tin-opener

oar

Oliver **O**ctopus has many objects to show. He often forgets to take
off his **o**vercoat in the classroom. He played an **o**ld lullaby **o**n his **o**boe.

P p

plant

patch

pot

pocket

pink pants

petals

Peter Puppy put a sunflower plant in his pocket.
He pointed at it.

Q q

whole pie

1 2
3

quarter piece
4

Please be quiet, children. Oswald Owl has a question
to ask you. "How many quarter pieces of pie are
there in one whole pie?" You are quite right! Each
whole pie can be divided into four quarters.

R r

rose

left foot

left hand

ribbon

right foot

rug

Ruth Rabbit has a ribbon in her hair.
She has a rose in her left hand.
Huckle has a ribbon under his right foot.
Bugdozer is rolling up the rug.

Spotty Leopard showed his **s**choolmates a tube of paste. He **s**queezed it. It **s**quirted. It made a **s**pot. Paste is **s**ticky. Miss Honey told **S**potty to get some **s**oap and water.

Tom **T**iger told everyone how to **t**ie a knot. He **t**ook **t**wo pieces of **t**wine and **t**ied them **t**ogether.

Ursula Pig stays **u**nder her **u**mbrella when it rains. She has **u**sed it a lot.

Victor Bear showed some pretty **v**iolets and a **v**ine in a **v**ase. He tripped on the **v**ine.

Willy Fox can't think of one word that beings with a 'W'. Can you help him?

W w

watch

What am I? I'm a worm wagon! Watch me wiggle!

wheel

X x

Lowly showed the class how he plays the **x**ylophone with one foot.

Y y

Yvonne dropped an egg on the floor so everyone could see the **y**ellow **y**olk inside.

Z z

zig zag

Lowly walked **z**igzag.

"Very good!" said Miss Honey. "Now, let us all recite our ABC's! Begin!"

"ABCD... EFG... HIJK... LMN... O.P. QRS... TUV... W... X.. Y.. Z

Now I've said my ABC's, tell me what you think of me"

Making Things

Miss Honey showed us how to make all kinds
of exciting things with a few simple
materials and tools.

embroidery

needle

thread

weaving

Kathy embroidered
with a needle and thread.

Penny is a weaver.
She wove a table mat.

paste

magazine

scrapbook

crayon

colouring book

Huckle cut up pictures out of old
magazines and made a scrapbook.

Charlie coloured a colouring
book with crayons.

knitting bobbin

Frances knitted a pullover for Lowly.

stringing beads

Ruth strung beads on a string.

modelling clay

Willy modelled a bunny with modelling clay.

building blocks

Robert built a tower with building blocks.
Stop Robert! That is enough!

making things
with paper

paper aeroplanes

Mary cut out pieces of paper and
folded them up. She made a doll house.

Arthur folded paper, too. He made paper aeroplanes.
ARTHUR PIG! You know better than to throw things in class!

Playtime in the Playground

Every day the children have a short time for play.
When the weather is nice they play in the playground.

swing

rings

sliding pole

climbing ladder

shovel

pail

sand box

barrel

hurt knee

hide and seek

kicking a ball

ring-a-ring-a-rosie

marbles

jacks

see-saw

slide

ring toss

leap frog

catching a ball

skipping rope

pat-a-cake

hop scotch

stilts

The Days of the Week

Sunday Monday Tuesday Wednesday Thursday Friday Saturday

At school, Miss Honey teaches us many things.
When she is not teaching, she is very busy doing other things.

On **Sunday** afternoon, she drove out into the country with her friend
Mr Bruno to have a picnic. Picnics are always fun. Don't you think so?

On **Monday** after school, she did her washing.

On **Tuesday** morning before school, she baked
a cake for the sick children in the hospital.

Mother Cat took it to them.

On **Wednesday** she made up packages of used clothing to send to children who do not have enough to wear.

On **Thursday** she met the headmaster and the other teachers to plan a school picnic.

On **Friday** she went to the library to read books and study. She is always learning new things to teach the children.

On **Saturday** she did her shopping. And on Saturday night she invited Mr Bruno to supper. He always brings flowers when he visits her.

You are a very busy lady, Miss Honey!

LEARNING TO COUNT

0 1 2 3 4 5
zero one two three four five

6 7 8 9 10
six seven eight nine ten

"Now we shall learn how to count," said Miss Honey.
"Huckle will hold the card showing the correct answer.
How many children are sitting on the stool?" she asked.
The answer is **none**. There is no one sitting there.
We use the figure **zero** to show **none**.

How many flowers are in the vase on
Miss Honey's desk? You are right, Huckle.
There is just **one** flower.

When those little girls stop talking,
how many quiet little girls will there be?
There will be **two** quiet little girls
when they stop talking.

Roger Raccoon drew a picture of the teacher,
a picture of Huckle, and a picture of Lowly.
If you say he drew **three** pictures, you are right!

Arthur Pig had some big marbles in his pocket.
His pocket ripped open and they fell out.
One, two, three, four. Four bouncing marbles.

Miss Honey asked Willy Fox to take the wastepaper baskets out and
empty them. But, Willy don't take them all out at once! Empty the
five wastepaper baskets one at a time! One, two, three, four, **five**.

Well, what a mess Willy made! How many
brooms did the class use to clean it up?
Six brooms is the right answer.

Now, why are all those children raising their hands? It's because they want to ask Miss Honey
for permission to go to the cloakroom. You always have to ask, you know. "All right, you may go.
But hurry back," said the teacher. **Seven** children left the room to go to the lavatory.

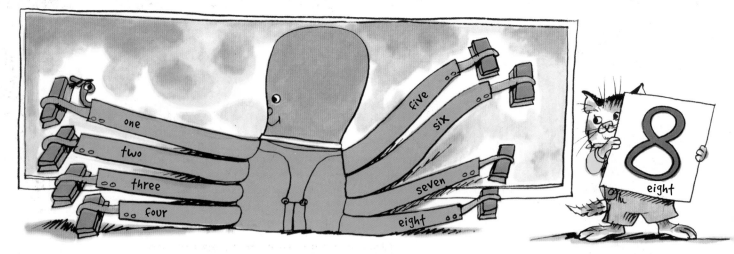

Miss Honey asked Oliver to wipe the chalk off the blackboard with the dusters.
How many dusters did he use? He has **eight** arms so he used **eight** dusters.

By the time the blackboard was wiped
clean, the dusters were full of chalk dust.
Miss Honey asked some children to clap the dusters
to clean them. How many are clapping dusters?

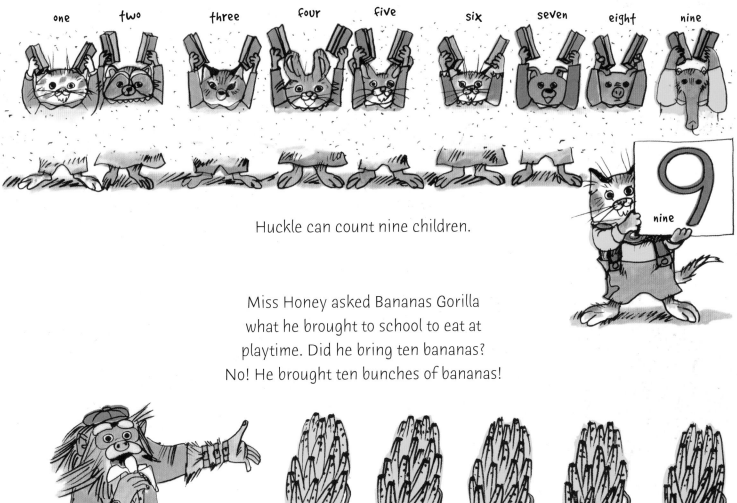

one   two   three   four   five   six   seven   eight   nine

Huckle can count nine children.

nine

9

Miss Honey asked Bananas Gorilla
what he brought to school to eat at
playtime. Did he bring ten bananas?
No! He brought ten bunches of bananas!

one   two   three   four   five

six   seven   eight   nine   ten

10

My he does like bananas!
Now let us all count from **one** to **ten**.
One, two, three, four, five, six, seven, eight, nine, ten.
Very good, children!

The Hours of the Day

It was Saturday. There was no school.
But there were lots of things for Huckle to do.
His friend Lowly was coming to spend the day
with him. He was going to stay overnight, too.

At **7** o'clock Huckle bounced out of bed.

At **8** o'clock he ate his breakfast. Father Cat
took the tablecloth to work with him again.

At **9** o'clock he tidied his room.

At **10** o'clock he went shopping for food.

At **11** o'clock he played in his muddy yard with Lowly. He fell down a few times.

12 o'clock is noontime, Huckly and Lowly ate their lunches. Lowly remembered to take his hat off at the table.

At **1** o'clock they both lay down and had a nap.

At **2** o'clock they went for a ride.
They bumped into Joe, the school caretaker.
He was on his way to school
and was late again.

At **3** o'clock they walked home.

At **4** o'clock they watched television.

At **5** o'clock
Father Cat came home.

At **6** o'clock Mother Cat served a
surprise for supper. She served
Huckle's guest first.

At **7** o'clock Father Cat gave
Huckle and Lowly their baths.
"Where did that soap go?"
asked Father Cat.

At **8** o'clock Father Cat read them
a bedtime story in bed.

And at **9** o'clock they were sound asleep.
Sleep tight, Huckle! Sleep tight, Lowly!

Miss Honey's Busy Helpers

Everyone helps in little ways to make Miss Honey's life happier.
Miss Honey will never forget the day when Lowly polished her apple.

That same day Roger opened the window
and the papers blew away.

Arthur closed the door so that
they wouldn't escape.

Miss Honey remembers that Huckle
sharpened the pencils that day.
He made them a little too short.

Patsy picked up
papers off the floor and put
them in the wastepaper basket.

Eddie cleaned
the blackboard.

Peter washed the
blackboard with a sponge.

Bobby clapped the dusters.
Miss Honey was about to tell him
to clean them outside when…

…she saw that someone was watering her plant!

"STOP IT!" she cried.

Why, it was another of her busy helpers!
Joe the caretaker! He had been washing
the outside of the windows.
"Did you get a little wet?" he asked.
"You forgot to tell someone
to close the window!"
OH, JOE! You should have looked!

Shapes

"Everything has a shape," said Miss Honey.
"I will show you different kinds of shapes.
First, look at my shape. Mr Bruno says I have
a beautiful shape. Would you say that I am
fatter or **thinner** than Lowly?
Yes! I am a little bit **fatter** than Lowly."

Lowly has been eating peas.
Peas are round in shape.

A ball is round, too.
But Lowly isn't able to eat that.

A block has a square shape.

An egg is oval-shaped.

The moon is sometimes crescent-shaped.

Oh, yes! Someone sent me a Valentine
in the shape of a heart.
Can you guess who sent it?

To Miss Honey from Bruno

diamond

triangle

bell

circle

star

cone

I have asked Huckle to draw some
more shapes for you to see.

straight

curved

crooked

And also some lines. Thank you, Huckle.

Now some things change their shape.
A large candle becomes small.

large   small

A short seedling becomes
a tall sunflower.

tiny   great

IT'S MAGIC!

smoke

fire

wood

And a burning piece of wood turns to smoke and ashes.
Can you think of anything else that changes shape?
A snowman, maybe? When?

Drawing and Painting

Drawing and painting are always fun. On drawing and painting days, Miss Honey's class is always full of artists. Some artists draw pictures with crayons or pencils. Some paint pictures with paint and water. All of them wear smocks so that they won't get their clothes messy.

Huckle helped the teacher pass out the drawing and painting materials.

These are some of the things he handed to the other artists.

pencils

rubber

ball-point pen

pencil sharpener

marker pen

crayons

paint jars

water dish

mixing tray

pastels

paint box

paint brush

At last everyone was ready.

Mildred Hippo placed a pad of paper on her easel. She drew an insect with her pencil.

easel

Elizabeth Rabbit drew a picture with her pastels. She pinned it on the wall.

My Doll

Arthur Pig painted a red apple on the paper.

paint   water

picture

Bobby Cat painted some red footprints on the floor.

Roger Raccoon went to the sink to wash the dirty paint water out of his water dish.
He ran the water too hard.
He made a spatter painting.

sink

My! What a busy group of artists!

Colours

Huckle will show some of the things he has painted.

Red

apple · strawberry · fire engine · heart · the inside of a watermelon

He has painted pictures of some **red** things…

orange · orange · pumpkin · carrot · bus · goldfish

…and some **orange** things.

Yellow

daffodil · banana · corn · lemon · cheese · bell

Yellow is a bright sunny colour.

Green

peas · leaf · blades of grass · insect · clover leaf · lettuce · pine tree · the outside of a watermelon

Many things are green. Some insects are **green**.

BUGDOZER

Blue

cloud sky

blueberries

bluebells

yacht

Huckle painted a **blue** sky.
When it is cloudy, the sky is
coloured grey. Be careful, Huckle

Violet or Purple

violet

plum

pansy

thistle

grapes

Huckle painted the floor **violet**.
Purple is almost the same colour as violet.

Brown

walnut

potato

chocolate
Easter Bunny

shoelace

light dark

Colours can be light or dark. A potato is **light brown**.
A chocolate Easter bunny is **dark brown**.

Black

doorbell

gumdrop

tyre

hat

White

egg

snowman

He painted some **black** things…

…and some white ones.

Besides painting pictures, Huckle painted himself.
Wash the paint off, Huckle, and put on a clean smock. Thank you!

"Now, Huckle," said Miss Honey, "will you please write all the letters of the alphabet? I want all the children to copy them. With a little help, maybe they will be able to write their own names."

sharpen your pencil!

Aa Bb Cc Dd

Aa Bb Cc Dd

Ee Ff Gg Hh

Ee Ff Gg Hh

Ii Jj Kk Ll

Ii Jj Kk Ll

Mm Nn Oo Pp

Mm Nn Oo Pp

Qq Rr Ss Tt

Qq Rr Ss Tt

Uu Vv Ww Xx

Uu Vv Ww Xx

Yy Zz

Yy Zz

Now, everyone, please take a pencil and paper and try to write your own name.

In **June** Miss Honey asked Joe to fix a table.
One leg wobbled a bit.

Well, he really fixed that table, didn't he?
You can fix it correctly during our summer holidays.
We will see you in the autumn. Keep the school
looking nice, Joe!

In **July**, when everyone
was away on holiday,
Joe gave everything
a fresh coat of paint.

The month of **August** is very hot and sunny. That's when Joe fixed the showers in the gym. He pretended he was at the seashore.

In **September** school begins. Joe made a new cement pavement for the children to walk on. It is now soft and wet. Tomorrow it will be hard and dry. I think you should have made it a few days sooner, Joe!

nice work, Joe!

In **October**, the leaves begin to fall. Joe raked them up and carried them in his wheelbarrow to a big pile. He burned them in an open place so that nothing else would catch fire.

I love the smell of burning leaves!

JOE! You left the wheelbarrow too close to the fire!

November is a cold and windy month. Winter is coming. Joe sawed the dead branches off the trees so that they wouldn't be broken off by the wind and fall on top of something. The headmaster came out to look at his new car.

In **December** there are lots of holiday celebrations. Joe put up the school Christmas tree. He decorated it with ornaments. It looks beautiful. So far Joe has done something right. He only has to put the star on the top of the tree. Can you reach it, Joe?

The School Library

Now, where was Miss Honey taking the children?
She was taking them to the school library!
She was going to read stories to them
out of some library books.

The library shelves were full of all kinds of books.
Miss Honey gathered her children around and read some exciting stories.

She read a fairy tale about a pretty
princess and a brave knight.
The knight had a fight with a dragon.

She told them a story about a little Eskimo boy
who lived in an igloo far away in the cold North.
An igloo is a house made of blocks of ice.

"Look at the picture of the Eskimo
boy paddling his kayak in the
water," said Miss Honey.

When she finished reading, Miss Honey said, "Any child who
can write his or her name on a library card will be able
to take a book home to read!"

Miss Honey took a rubber stamp and stamped a date
in Huckle's book. Now he will know on what day he must
return the book to the library. The other children waited
their turn to borrow a book. Huckle rode home
on the school bus. Mother Cat
was waiting for him.

Huckle showed her his library card. She was so pleased
to find that Huckle could write his own name!

"Huckle! You are really learning a lot in school!" she said.
Huckle hurried into the house to read his book.

Now, at least once every school year,
Miss Honey takes the children on a school picnic.
Mr Bruno was invited, too. He cooked the hot dogs.
Miss Honey poured the lemonade.

Bananas Gorilla played his Banana Guitar.
Huckle scooped out the ice cream.
Joe brought his kite and showed everyone how to fly it.
And a very good time was had by one and all!

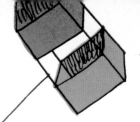

FINISH LINE